Into a Book

Just Right Reader

"Did you ever want to jump into a book?" Bert asked his sister. "Like when a person in the book could use some help?"

"I would enter as a hero in a cape!" offered Summer.

"I could help the mother, father, sister, and brother find shelter in the storm!"

"You'd better yell and holler!" said Summer. "It could be thundering."

"Look! That lemur's dinner fell off its perch," said Summer.

"I could tell the zoo person that the lemur looks stern," said Bert. "It needs to calm the lemur's nerves."

"The second graders are playing baseball. If I were, I could cover that spot if the ball is going over!" said Bert.

"You'll do a better job if you take your ball glove," Summer said, snickering.

"I prefer made-up tales," said Summer. "The prince is on his horse. He doesn't see the panther over in the forest."

"I would offer to enter on my horse and warn him," said Bert.

"The baker is about to lose the top of his cake. I could enter and put a platter under it," said Bert.

"Very good!" said Summer. "You'd better not eat it!"

"This is very nice art. It looks like Mister Sanders' farm," said Summer.

But no answer from Bert.

"Bert? Bert?"

Summer looked at the book. Bert was helping the farmer!

"How did Bert get into the book." pondered Summer.

Phonics Fun

- Go on a hunt for words with r-controlled er.
- Choose a book.
- Look through the book.
- Write down 5 words you find.
- Read the words to a friend.

Comprehension

How would this story change if it happened somewhere else?

High Frequency Words

there   very   where

Decodable Words

baker	over
Bert	panther
better	perch
brother	person
cover	platter
dinner	pondered
enter	prefer
ever	Sanders
farmer	shelter
father	sister
grader	snicker
holler	stern
Mister	Summer
mother	thunder
nerve	under
offer	